Also by Helen Frost

room 214

a year in poems

Helen Frost

room 214

a year in poems

SQUARE FISH • FARRAR STRAUS GIROUX • NEW YORK

J
FROST   10|14

SQUARE
FISH
An Imprint of Macmillan
175 Fifth Avenue
New York, NY 10010
mackids.com

Square Fish books may be purchased for business or promotional use. For information on bulk
purchases, please contact the Macmillan Corporate and Premium Sales Department at
(800) 221-7945 x 5442 or by e-mail at specialmarkets@macmillan.com.

The Library of Congress has cataloged the hardcover edition of this book as follows:
Frost, Helen, 1949–
    Spinning through the universe / Helen Frost.
        p.   cm.
    Summary: A collection of poems written in the voices of Mrs. Williams of room 214,
her students, and a custodian about their interactions with each other, their families, and
the world around them. Includes notes on the poetic forms represented.
    [1. Children—Fiction.   2. Schools—Fiction.   3. Interpersonal relations—
Fiction.   4. Family life—Fiction.   5. Poetry.]   I. Title.
PZ7.F9205 Sp 2004   [Fic]—dc21   2003048056

ISBN 978-1-250-04009-1 (paperback)

Originally published in the United States by Farrar Straus Giroux
First Square Fish Edition: 2014
Book designed by Barbara Grzeslo
Square Fish logo designed by Filomena Tuosto

10 9 8 7 6 5 4 3 2 1

AR: 3.5

Dedicated with love to Chad, Lloyd, and Glen

Contents

PART 2— Elm Trees

Room 214 is named for Valentine's Day, 2/14.
It is a room centered in love.

PART ONE

Great Explorers

Great Explorers, Room 214

MRS. WILLIAMS

I tape the children's pictures of the great explorers—Leif
Eriksson, Magellan, Sacagawea and York and Lewis and Clark—
on the wall around our big 3-D relief

map. Across the room, taped on windows, leaves from the park,
pressed between waxed paper, catch the light
the morning sun shines in. My work

starts early. It's never really done. Last night
the moon kept me awake and I
thought about these kids—what might

be on their minds? What makes them happy? Sad? Why
does Maria tear her papers into shreds?
What puts that twinkle in Jaquanna's eye?

I sometimes get the feeling that Eddie dreads
each school day. I wonder what's going on with Sam—
yesterday when they all put their heads

down, he fell asleep in seconds flat. Why did Andrew slam
his math book shut, the other day when I came in?
Does Rosa have warm clothes? Does Dustin understand

the work we're doing? And then there's Ben,
so happy whenever his team's
winning, so miserable when

they lose. I write my plans: Reading—themes
of love and courage. Social studies—the explorers' dreams.

Sunlight, orange leaves,
their veins like veins in my hands—
leaves, light, hands, dancing.

NAOMI

Grandma Keeps Forgetting

VONDA

Grandma keeps forgetting that my grandpa died.
She asks us where he is, why he's been gone
so long. And if we say, *Remember?*

He had a heart attack, she tries to remember
but she can't. We have to tell her that he died.
That makes her mad. So now we say he's gone

to someplace nice. She's glad he hasn't gone
to war again. It wasn't always like this. I remember
once when I was little, we found a bird that died.

What's "died"? I asked, and Grandma said, *The bird is gone,*
but we remember.

Late Again

SAM

We got evicted yesterday. I came home and all my
stuff was in a box outside the door.
Me, my mom, my sister, and her baby, Ty,
had to sleep in my mom's brother's car.
I'm late again. I hope nobody asks me why.

It's hard to sleep with so much traffic going by.
There's no alarm clock in my uncle's car.
My clothes are dirty. I couldn't comb my hair. I
know the kids are thinking, *You're
late again.* At least nobody's asking why.

Should I make up a story? They'll guess it's a lie,
and anything I'd say, they've heard before.
It's hard to get my work done, but I'll try.
Sometimes Mrs. Williams lets me sleep. So far
she hasn't said, *You're late again. Why?*

Without My Bike

JON

My bike is blue. Black stripes. And now it's gone.
I want to know who took it. Why? And where?

My bike is part of me. We're like the wind
together, going anywhere we want.

Without my bike, my legs are empty. It
has tricks you have to know to ride it right,

like: jerk the handlebars before you jump,
and push them down again to get more speed.

It's like my bike and me are brothers. Friends
that never fight. A new one wouldn't be

the same. I want my own bike back. It's blue.
Black stripes. It whistles when you go real fast.

Make a Few Adjustments
ANDREW

Jon just left his bike lying in the street
like he don't care. Anybody could've stole it.
I ain't no thief, but I'm the one that took
it home. I gotta fix that squeaky noise it makes.
Can't stand it! You get yourself a bike,
you should take care of it. I wonder

if Jon knows how the derailleur works. Wonder
if he ever greases it. He rides down the street
like he thinks he got some kinda magic bike,
then he leaves it lying outside in the rain! I know he's
     missing it—
I'll put it back tomorrow, after I make
a few adjustments. Let him think somebody took

it, for real—maybe he'll start taking
better care of it. Lately I been wondering
if you can make
a living fixing bikes. There's a dude on my street
that can drive a car one block and tell you what it
needs to make it run right. I can do that with bikes,

but not so many people need their bikes
fixed. So, I don't know—Dad says, *Keep taking*

math. He knows I'm good at it,
but my teachers never see that. I wonder
what Mrs. Williams meant: *Andrew, you're a one-way street—*
that thing she said when she was trying to make

me tell her why I slammed my book shut. (Not *make*
me, exactly. She just asked.) The day I rode Jon's bike
home, I found $20 in the street.
I put it in my math book, just taking
care of it, that's all. But I been wondering
what she meant by *one-way street*. Maybe it

means I don't tell her what I'm thinking. It
gets to be a habit. Last year, my teacher made
me mad—so suspicious all the time. Wonder
why he didn't like me. His voice sounded like Jon's bike—
faster he talked, higher it got. But I take
Mrs. Williams's point. I could maybe open up my "street"

a little. Tell her I want to take that test for Gifted—wonder
if I'm smart enough. Some ways, yes—like, I can make bikes
out of parts. Got one now, ready for its test run on the street.

Black/orange flower
flying, lands on a dark branch—
monarch butterfly.

NAOMI

Suki

RYAN

Suki's gone. Our cat.
I looked in the hall closet.
The cellar. Nowhere.

We've had her almost three years.
She wouldn't just leave. Would she?

∞

Three days. I won't cry.
Her bed empty by the door.
All our rooms quiet.

Who would think one missing cat
could make a whole house silent?

Pepperoni Was My Dog

RICHARD

I know how Ryan feels. Suki, his white cat—she's

Missing. He wants me to help him look, but
I don't know his cat. I don't know where
Suki sleeps or what she eats. In other words,
Suki isn't Pepperoni.

Pepperoni was my dog. He died. Now
Every day when I come home from school,
Pepperoni doesn't thump his tail.
Pepperoni doesn't curl beside me on the couch,
Even if I whistle and pat the place he likes.
Rawhide bones and chewed up toys aren't left all
Over the back yard. My ears are empty from the
Noises Pepperoni doesn't make.
I know how much space one cat or dog can fill.

Suki

RYAN

She came home! She ate
and left again. I followed.
She's under the porch.

You can hear something in there.
Suki lies down, curls up—purrrrrrr

∞

Four kittens! Two white
like Suki. One gray and brown.
One black as midnight.

You have to lift a loose board
to see them. Careful, don't touch!

∞

Midnight. Small white star
above his right eye. Suki
lets me pick him up.

I hold his fur to my cheek.
His heart beats against my skin.

One Small Kitten
MANUEL

Now what do we want with a cat?
That's all my mama got to say.
She won't listen. I tell her that
it's just a kitten, brown and gray.

Ryan says I can have it when
it's big enough to give away.
Mama says *No!* I say again,
Just a small kitten, brown and gray.

I know a good place to keep it—
a box in the downstairs hallway.
I measured, and the box will fit
my soft-eyed kitten, brown and gray.

*You got four sisters! There's enough
mouths to feed! Now who's going to pay
for cat food?* But—it won't eat much.
Just one kitten. It's brown and gray

and it likes me. It licks my hand
with its sandpaper tongue. Someday
I'll have a big house, just me and
my own kitten. Soft, brown, and gray.

Who, Me?

JAQUANNA

The music teacher said, *Jaquanna—*
stand here and sing.
He didn't say Shaquina or Johanna.
I didn't do anything

but stand there and sing
and he knew my name.
I didn't do anything
wrong, we just came

in and he knew my name.
You think we come every day?
Wrong. We just came
three times before. Hey—

He didn't say Shaquina or Johanna.
The music teacher said Jaquanna!

Her Thick Black Hair
LAURA

My mom has breast cancer.
My brother Tom says she might die.
I ask her. She just says, *I'm going to do*
everything I can to stay alive. You
kids are my best medicine. I
love you. That's her answer!

Not what I want to hear. I know it's true,
but I want *No!* Not *I will try.*
She's my mom! A dancer!
She sings with her hands. Her
thick black hair is falling out. My
hair is black like hers. I'm a dancer too.

Dark branches, blue sky,
dew drops on a spider's web—
spider in the center.

NAOMI

It's Hard to Fit In

SHAWNA

It's hard to fit in with these girls. I see
them whispering together in the hall
and then when I walk by, they stop, like they're all
perfect and something's wrong with me.
My name is Shawna Laird, but Natalie
says "Ton o' Lard." Huge joke. I know they all
laugh at me behind my back—too tall,
too fat—whatever. And no one better be
the friend of anyone who's not like them.
They act like they're all following some rule
written somewhere I don't know about:
if you're nice to Shawna, that's the end
of sleeping over, going to the pool.
Be like us, and if you aren't—Keep Out.

KATE

Do I have to be like this to keep out
of Natalie's way? Is she the boss of everyone?
I hate how she's been calling Shawna "Ton
o' Lard"! I don't care if Shawna's *stout*
as Mom would say. But no one is about
to challenge Natalie. It's like she won
some contest, and now she gets to tell the sun
who it should shine on. She gets that little pout
on her face, and everyone does what she says,
even if they think she's wrong. I
sat with Shawna on the bus last week.
She's nice. She makes me laugh. But two days
later, when Natalie was teasing her, why
did I just stand there like I can't speak?

ROSA

I just stand there like I can't speak
English, like last year when I first came
to America. Natalie—that same
girl that's teasing Shawna this week—
kept saying *Cómo está frijole?* Monique
would laugh. Get it—*how you BEAN?* So lame,
I know, but—every day! Don't blame
me if I didn't *turn the other cheek*
like the Bible says. No way. I fought
back with my fists. The principal sent me home,
and kids and teachers still think I'm so
mean. I'm not mean. I'm nice. But I'm not
going to fight for Shawna. She's on her own
like I was. I still miss Mexico.

NATALIE

Like she was Little Miss Mexico
or something, one time last year Rosa hit me just
because I said something in Spanish. Big fuss
about that. Can't people take a joke?
Now Shawna. When I heard we got to go
to the museum on an air-conditioned bus,
I thought Kate would sit with me. She must
have known—I always sit with her! But no—
I get on the bus, and there's Kate
already sitting next to Shawna. I had
to sit alone, two rows behind them. They
were laughing the whole time. I really hate
that. So I tease Shawna about being fat.
I can't help it if my mind works that way.

I can't help it. I mind that Dad works far away.
He's like those butterflies that Rosa saw
in Mexico. Once she tried to draw
them for me—millions in the sky one day,
millions in the trees. But then they
all flew off. I wish there was a law
to make my dad come home. Back on McGraw
Street, he'd sit in his blue chair and play
his banjo while I went to sleep.
If I close my eyes, I almost hear
those songs again. Since he left and Mom
got married and he moved, I keep
wishing he'd come back, or we'd move there.
It won't happen. Dad's not coming home.

MONIQUE

It won't happen. Dad's not coming home
for my birthday. He can't get any leave
at least till after New Year's. Uncle Steve
says he'll help with my party. Right. Come
in his hippie clothes and tell his dumb
jokes. Pull a quarter from my sleeve
with that grin on his face, and give
it to me like it's twenty dollars. Some
party. No way. Who should I invite?
Natalie, of course. And Kate. Jaquanna. Not
Rosa, not Shawna—they don't get along
with Natalie. Maybe Chrystal. And I might
invite the new girl to find out what
she's like. I'm not a snob. Don't get me wrong.

ASHA

She's like, *I'm not a snob, don't get me wrong,*
and then she says who I'm supposed to like
and who I shouldn't talk to. Who got their bike
at Goodwill, who beat up who last year—this long
story. I don't care! I like Shawna.
Rosa seems okay. Why does Monique
care about Natalie's new Nikes?
I've never had a dad. My mom ran a pawn-
shop that just went out of business. What
does that make me? A nobody? The *new
girl* for the "Friends of Natalie"
to ignore, or—if I'm really lucky—not.
I just want someone to say, *Hi, who are you?*
It's hard to fit in with these girls I see.

What's that squirrel doing?
Naomi, pay attention!
Nose twitch—tail swish—gone . . .

NAOMI

Recess

ANTOINE

Free for twenty minutes!
We can run! We can yell!
Dodgeball, kickball, poison tag—
Come on—let's get outside!

No one tells us what to do.
Free for twenty minutes!
Drop my pencil, close my book,
think whatever thoughts I want.

Hey, Ben, you be captain.
Pick me, pick Sam and Vonda!
Free for twenty minutes!
I got the ball—come on!

One time I opened up my pen,
a little spring shot out.
That's how I feel at recess,
Free for twenty minutes!

Ten

My Dad's father died when Dad was ten,
and Grandma gave him his dad's Red Sox cap.
Like Dad and me, my grandpa was named Ben.

Now I'm ten, and I'm a Red Sox fan.
When Dad gets home, he says, *Let's play catch!*
Even though his father died when he was ten,

Dad remembers playing ball when
his dad came home. They knew all the stats,
like Dad and me. Since Grandpa was named Ben,

they called Dad Benny, and his father Ben.
Sometimes Dad calls me Benny, like we're going back
in time. Dad's father died when he was ten,

but I keep thinking how it could have been—
Dad pitching, Grandpa catching, me up at bat,
Grandpa, Dad, and me, all named Ben.

I never used to think about this. Then
Dad gave me my grandpa's Red Sox cap!
He's had it since his father died, when he was ten.
Dad says he wishes I'd known Grandpa Ben.

Bottom Line

DUSTIN

My dad says, *Nothing matters more than grades.*
It's like in business: What's the bottom line?
Whatever it takes, you do what you have to do.

It might be wrong to cheat, but it's not hard.
I drop my pencil, lean across my desk,
and glance to see what answers Vonda picked.

By chance, I'll pick the answers Vonda picked.
I grab my pencil, lean back to my test.
It might be wrong to cheat, but it's not hard.

Whatever it takes, I do what I have to do.
Like my dad's business: What's the bottom line?
My dad says nothing matters more than grades.

My People

JACK

Our social studies book tells what the Indians *did*,
not what we *do*. It sounds like they don't know

we still exist. Pinch me. I'm not
extinct, like a dinosaur. My people didn't go

west on the Trail of Tears and then just disappear.
Some of us survived. Not everyone, no,

but my mom says, *Just watch, we're
going to bring the old ways back.* My uncles know

our dances, and they're teaching me. We still
have lots of songs and stories. When my toe

got infected, Grandma knew a way to heal it. Here
in school, I don't talk about that stuff. (People are so

ignorant.) But inside, where I'm sad and strong
and funny, all mixed up together, an old crow

keeps me company. He looks out at the world and
tells me things. He says: grow

up smart both ways, Indian and whiteman. I'm proud
of this A+ on Unit I. And I know things the teacher doesn't know

Friend

SHARRELL

What should I do?
Maria told me not to tell.
What should I do?
Her arms are bruised. She has these two
red hand prints on her back. *I fell,*
she says, but then she asks, *Sharrell,*
what should I do?

The Truth

MARIA

When I was small, he'd hit my mom. I'd hide
until he stopped, and then we'd all
pretend she wasn't hurt.
Then came a time
when he
hit me.
A lot. Now I'm
supposed to keep my shirt
pulled down so no one sees. *Stand tall,*
the teacher says. *Tell me what's on your mind.*
I'm like a turtle, head pulled deep inside
my shell. I hope she doesn't call
on me. What if I blurt
the truth sometime?
Here: see—
Help me.
Yes, it's a crime.
But if I tell—alert
someone—they'll send my dad to jail.
So I'm quiet, trying to decide.

Just Try
EDDIE

I sit
here wishing I
was smart enough to learn
to read. When it's my turn
she'll say, *Just try,*
but it

don't make
no sense to me.
I read like I'm in first
grade. I know I'm the worst
reader here. "D."
"Mistake."

That's all
I'll ever hear.
Two more kids. Then me. I'll
try to get sent out while
I can. *Safe there.*
The hall.

The Bluebird Zoo

MATTHEW

About that thing the teacher tells the
Bluebirds (our reading group—she
Calls us that, but everyone knows "Bluebirds" means
"Dumb Group")—she gets all serious and says,
Every day during reading, someone's mean to Eddie.
For once, let's try to read the whole story without
Getting distracted. You
Have a right to learn.
I want to help you. Well, it won't happen
Just 'cause she wants it to.
Kids don't like to be in Eddie's group. It makes it
Look like we're as slow as he is. We
Might not be the smartest kids, but we're
Not all like Eddie.
Okay—here's how I see it. Some
People, like Eddie, would rather just keep
Quiet. They don't like to
Read out loud. So when the teacher
Says it's going to be their
Turn, they make some kind of trouble. Eddie
Usually shoots a spitball at someone like
Veronica, who jumps up and starts a fight. Mrs.
Williams looks up, sees the commotion, sends both kids out.
Exactly what Eddie wants. The teacher's trying, but I bet this
Year will be like last year in the Bluebird
Zoo. I wish I was a Eagle.

Out in the Hall
VERONICA

Out in the hall with Eddie, him on one side, me on the other, I get as mad as a hissing cat. The place on my cheek where his spitball hit me burns like a blister.

After a while, we look at each other. He grins, I start to laugh. My cheek burns again, but different. Like someone kissed it and ran away. Quick, without looking back.

Room 214, 11 p.m.

MR. CARLSON

I save room 214 for last,
come in when all the halls are clean,
the gym floor mopped. I do that pretty fast,
then take my time in here, sit in the big green
chair in the reading corner, relax,
drink a cup of coffee. I don't mean
to be nosy, but I find things on the floor
and think about them. Just outside the door

tonight I found a paper heart with "Eddie"
written on one side. On the other
side, a purple *V*. These kids thinking about love already?
I know some of their parents. Dustin's mother—
I remember her from high school. She went steady
with a football player from another
school that was always beating us.
Sam's family is having a hard time. Russ

Pirney's little girl, Monique, is in this class.
I heard his unit was shipped overseas.
That's tough for kids, no weekend pass.
Here, on Vonda's desk, a picture of Louise
Jones—my old teacher—in her wheelchair on the grass
outside the nursing home. "Love from Grandma." Hard to
    believe

she's so old now. I had a good year
in her room, same age as the kids in here.

Wish I could make the whole
world safe for these kids. I can't
do that, so I just do my job. Roll
up the maps, water the plant
by the window. Jon told me someone stole
his bike, and then I heard that his aunt
found it on the playground. Who knows
how it got there? One of those

things where I just say, good,
something I don't have to think about,
it worked out like it should.
I've never been the sort to shout
about the problems of the world. If I could,
I'd give every kid a bike, take them out
to ball games. But I can't. I pick up my broom
and give them, one day at a time, a clean room.

PART TWO
Elm Trees

Ice covers each branch
like diamond bracelets. Bow down:
I crown thee—Queen Tree.

NAOMI

Elm Trees

MRS. WILLIAMS

Last night, Monique's mother called, and I went
Over to their house. Monique's father has been killed. It's
Very hard. I remember when the city cut down a beautiful
Elm tree on our street ten years ago. A huge

Absence filled our neighborhood—that's how their house feels
Now. Somehow I have to help the children understand his
Death, and how to offer comfort to Monique. These

Children have become so dear to me.
Oh, they fuss and argue with each other, and with me,
        sometimes—
Until something like this happens. Then they
Rise to their full strength
And gather round whoever needs their
Goodness. They make me think of
Elm tree saplings, spreading their new branches.

Crying

NATALIE

Mrs. Williams told us, *Monique lost her father.* What?!
You don't *lose* a person, like Ryan lost his cat.

Monique's dad got killed, is what happened.
I'd rather say things straight out.
Now everybody's talking about Monique, her
Dad, and "fighting for our country." I don't even

Want to talk about it.
One time I slept over at her house, I
Remember her dad made us this great breakfast. I
Know I should say something nice, but nice
Seems stupid now. At recess, I couldn't think of anything

To say and I just blurted out,
He was so great! I really liked your dad!
And then I started crying like a big baby.
That's when Monique grabbed my hand and held on tight.

We got out of there,
Away from everyone. I found out
You don't have to talk to be a friend.

Waffles

MONIQUE

Dad. My dad. Not Sergeant Pirney. Everyone's been saying he's
A hero because he
Died protecting our country. One lady
Said *I'm* a hero for giving him to America.

No! I didn't give him up! I never got to say
One single word about it! And now
They act like I'm the one who

Commanded him to go.
(Oh, Dad, I wanted you to be a hero *here*!)
Mom understands. She asked me
If I want the flag from his coffin.
Not right now. Wasn't it the flag that made him
Go away and get killed? Mom just

Hugs me. She doesn't make me act like I'm
Okay. She knows how it is. Yesterday we tried
Making waffles, like Dad used to every Sunday.
Each of us made one. Then Mom ate mine and I ate hers.

Perfect

SHAWNA

Langston Hughes wrote a poem I like.
It says "Life for me ain't been no crystal stair."
Kids all seem to like that poem,
Even though it's about an old woman.

The woman's life is
Hard, but she keeps climbing up those stairs. Maybe
Everyone's life has something hard.
You know? Like Monique's dad. I
Really thought Monique's life must be easy.
Everything about her seems so perfect.

All her nice clothes, her pretty hair,
Lots of friends. But now this.
Last night, I looked at my dad

Playing with my little sister, Emily. Laughing with his
Eyes, he held up two fingers behind my sister's head:
>   *How many, how many, ol' Cow Pluck,*
>   *Pretty good girl, but she had bad luck.*
>   *How many fingers do I hold up?*
Remember, he said, *how we played this game when you were*
Four? I grinned at Dad, and he and
Emily both smiled back. I remember lots of games like Ol'
Cow Pluck. I'm . . . lucky. Who would have thought
That I'm the one whose life is perfect?

Oh—a woodpecker—
Rat-a-tat! Rat-a-tat-tat!
Bright red on its head.

NAOMI

At the Shelter

SAM

I don't mind living at the shelter.
There's fourteen ladies and twelve kids
Staying in a big brick house. We all

Have to promise not to talk
About each other, so I don't say that
Rosa used to live there till her
Dad got a job and

They moved back with him. Mom says we're
Only going to be there a few weeks, till she

Gets back on her feet. One lady at the shelter always says,
Eat your vegetables, Sam. She used to be a
Teacher, and sometimes she helps me with

My homework. She won't give me the answers, just
Yes, that's right, or, *Try again.* Mrs.

Williams is surprised to see how
Organized I am. See, there was this
Red backpack, almost new, that some
Kid left behind and they said I can have it. I

Do my homework, put it in the backpack, then put the
    backpack
On a hook by the door. Now, if Ty wakes up and cries at
Night, I get right back to sleep.
Every day this week, I got to school on time.

In the Middle
CHRYSTAL

My mom has a new baby named
O'Shondra. Her little brown fingers wrap around
Mine, and her black curls are so soft. But

Grandpa said he won't be her grandpa. He'll
Only be mine. I can't believe he said
That. It's because

My sister is biracial and Grandpa's prejudiced. Mom
Argued with him. Her face got all
Red, and she said she didn't
Really want to be his daughter if he felt that way.
I just stood there in the middle, loving
Everyone. O'Shondra was the only one smiling. I
Don't want her to find out about this.

The Answer
ANDREW

This time I got
A+ in math. Dad just said, *I*
Know, when he saw my report card: *Andrew is*
Exceptionally talented, Mrs. Williams wrote.

The way she found out was, we do these s'posed-to-be-
Hard mental math problems. Like,
An example is: *One hundred times one hundred,*
Then, real quick, *Divided by nine.*

The whole class sits there,
Everyone trying to figure it out, but I just
See the answer, flashing in my mind. Like
That one—1111.111 . . . I see a row of dominoes going on

Forever. Last year, I got bad grades 'cause I'd never show my work
On paper. Or I'd do the steps in the wrong order—
Right answer, wrong way to get it.

Gifted class is tight.
I get to go as
Fast as I want, and every week
The teacher gives us Challenge Problems. I'm doing a project to
Explain the ratio of gears in a
Derailleur. (I think Jon figured out who fixed his bike.)

Every Day

LAURA

Thank you, thank you, thank you! I'm as
Happy as five birthdays at once. I'm as happy
As four snow days in a row and
Three pizza parties, put together!

When Mom got out of bed
And had breakfast with us, and then when
She took off her scarf and I saw

Her hair growing back, I couldn't
Even breathe, I was so happy.
Right now, I don't care if my brother is

Annoying. I don't care if
Naomi wins the art contest (like always).
So what if Vonda doesn't ask me to her party?
Who cares? I only care about one thing:
Every day my mom gives me a hug. It's like having
Recess all day, every day.

We Showed My Mom

SHARRELL

When Maria came to my house, crying,
Her lip was bleeding and her
Arm was black and blue. I
Took her in the kitchen and we

Showed my mom. She gave Maria a
Hug and put an ice pack
On her lip. Mom said she
Understood why Maria hadn't
Let us know about the way her
Dad was hurting her. *You need some help,* Mom said,

I'm going to call someone. I

Don't know what's going to happen next, but
One thing I'm sure of—I was right to tell my mom.

Fathers Can Learn
MARIA

When I went to Sharrell's house, her mom was
Home. She took one look at me
And blinked, like she might cry. But she didn't. She
Told me everything would be okay. I'm trying to believe her.

I thought they'd take me or my dad away. But I
Found out there's this class

I never knew about where fathers can learn to

Be nonviolent. The judge is
Letting Dad stay home, but he can't hurt
Us, and he has to keep going to those classes.
Right now, I still don't
Trust my dad. I keep my distance. He

Told Mom and me he wants to stay
Home and learn to be nicer. He said
Every time he hits us, he

Tells himself that's the last time. We'll see. Mom is
Ready to move out if Dad hurts
Us again, and Dad is trying not to. It's been
Three weeks and two days since he last
Hit me. My bruises don't show anymore.

Two robins nesting
almost hidden by new leaves.
No one else sees them.

NAOMI

Birthday Candles
MANUEL

This Saturday, my sister Nina
Has another birthday. She'll be eight.
Every year, Mama makes her cake
Real pretty and tells Nina she can
Eat however much she wants. But
See, Nina can't blow out her candles.

Even that big number kind.
Nina can't get her mouth into that
O shape. So one of us blows them out, and Mama picks
Up a piece of cake and tries to
Get some into Nina's mouth. Usually Nina loves it.
Her face lights up and she rocks back and forth.

Mama smiles. But last year, Nina spit
Out the cake. She started crying. Mama got
Up and left the room. I sat there
Thinking, *I bet Nina wants to blow out
Her own candles, like she sees us do.*
So this year, I have a plan. I

Think I can put a hair dryer
On her wheelchair, pointing at the cake. I

Figured out how to tape a flat board so one
Edge will hit the On switch when Nina hits the other
Edge with her arm. Then when she
Does that, she'll make the hair dryer blow out her candles!

Little League
BEN

Maybe we'll make it to the finals this year, maybe
Even win the league championship. We got our

Uniforms last night—red and white! I'm
Practicing different kinds of cursive *B*'s so I can sign

Autographs if the T-ball kids come to watch us in the
Tournament. Should I write messy or neat? Should I sign

"Ben" or "Benny"? Last night, me and Dad counted
All our Red Sox autographs—82—including Luis Tiant,
Ted Williams, Manny Ramirez, Carlton Fisk, and—Yaz!

Honor Roll

DUSTIN

I made the honor roll again.
That should make Dad and

Mom happy. Sometimes I wonder
If I could get good
Grades on my own. Do my
Homework without their help.
Take my tests without cheating.

But what if I try my best and
Everyone finds out I can't do the

Work? I'm not as smart as people think I am.
Really, I'm probably about average. I got a C
On the test I took that time Vonda was absent.
Nobody knows I cheat. I
Guess I'm not hurting anyone.

Hard Problem

KATE

Dustin was cheating.
One time I saw him look at Vonda's paper.

I started watching, and he did it a lot.

Hard problem. I thought
About what I should do. Tell
Vonda so she could cover up her answers?
Even if she did, he could cheat off someone else.

Tell Mrs. Williams? She'd know what to do.
Only thing was, I didn't want to

Be the one to get Dustin in trouble.
Every time I saw it, I felt worse. I really

Like Dustin. He's nice enough.
I think he could be smart if he tried. I was
Kind of scared, but here's what I did: I got Dustin's
E-mail address and asked him to

Tell his parents to put me on the list of friends
He can get mail from. Then I sent him a message:
I know you cheat. I won't tell, but you
Should stop. He didn't answer, but I think it worked.

Birds

MATTHEW

I love to watch birds fly.

When I'm alone outdoors,
It's like my eyes open up, and I
See birds everywhere. Even at night—I
Hear an owl hoot and I know where to look for it.

I know how to find all different kinds of nests.

When Mrs. Williams found out
About this, she got all happy and
Said, *Matthew, why don't you write about birds*

And how they build their nests?
No—I know I could,

Except then I might not see them
Anymore. I feel like, if I write about a
Great horned owl, or about hummingbirds, I'll
Lose whatever there's no words for. It's hard to
Explain, but I won't write about birds.

Boys

VONDA

Some girls talk about boys too much.
He's cute, or *He's a dork.* Veronica thinks
Eddie's like on MTV or something. If you

Ask me, boys are just a bunch of
Show-offs. If they win the spelling bee or
Kick a ball across the field, we're all
Supposed to notice. They don't seem to notice

Us when we do something great,
So I don't see why we should care

When they do. I
Hate talking about boys.
Even if they're nice
(Richard's okay, I guess), it's not like
Everything about them is so interesting.

Have you ever noticed how their
Ears stick out under their baseball caps?

I just want to go back to when we'd all
Say boys have cooties, and ignore them.

Girls

RICHARD

Why are girls so stupid?
Here I am, minding my own business,
End of a long day, getting on the bus.
Nothing on my mind but basketball.

I look up and there's Maria and Sharrell. Vonda

Coming right along behind them.
Oh, hi, Richard! they say. All three of them!
Man, they think they're so cute. I don't
Even answer, just pull my cap down,

Holler out to Ryan, *Hey,*
Over here! So Ryan sits with
Me and I don't have to look at those three girls,
Eating their Almond Joys and laughing.

Whispering About the Teacher
NAOMI

Now I see!
Asha whispered to me, out at recess,
Okay, I know it's rude, but don't you think
Mrs. Williams is getting kind of fat?
I saw right away what Asha meant—our teacher's

Pregnant! Not too much.
A lot of people wouldn't notice, but last
Year my mom and my

Aunt Rachel both had babies, and
They talked about it all the time.
They wore that kind of dress—
Empire waist, it's called—like I
Notice Mrs. Williams has just started wearing.
This probably won't mean we'll get a substitute;
It takes nine months to have a baby.
Only thing is, Mrs. Williams might get tired. Teachers can't
    take
Naps all the time, like my mom always did.

Brothers

ANTOINE

Those guys in the Civil War—
How could they kill their own brother?
I mean, you grow up in the same house—
North or South, either one. You play with the same
Kids—cousins, neighbors, church kids. Your dad prob'ly

Whups you if you fight too much. You
Have the same mom! She yells
At you one minute, kisses you
The next. So, these two brothers, say
Evan and Antoine, grow up together, somewhere like
Virginia. Then Evan moves to, say,
Erie, Pennsylvania. He writes home. Antoine
Reads his brother's letter, writes back.

The next thing they know, these President guys say,
Hey, dudes, we're going to war.
Okay, says Antoine in Virginia. *Sign me*
Up, says Evan, up in Erie. But I don't
Get this next part:
Here they are in different uniforms.
There's people dying all over the field.
So—they see each other.

If it was me and my brother

(Whose name happens to be Evan),
All I'd be thinking is, *Hey, man,*
Not today. Let's get on outta here.
This history we're reading is some weird stuff.

Families

ROSA

I was thinking about Sam. I asked
Mama, *Could we cook for them sometime?*

No, she said, *we barely got enough for us.*
Only then she started thinking, too, about the shelter.
They could come on Saturday, she said.

Mama made a lot of food—tacos,
Enchiladas, mole, sopaipillas—
And Sam's whole family came to our house.
Not just one time, either. Four times so far.

I'm pretty sure Sam doesn't have a dad.
My dad asked him, *You like fishing?* Sam said he

Never tried it. So now, every Sunday afternoon,
I see my dad get out two fishing poles. Sam
Comes over. Dad and Sam walk to the river. We
Eat fried fish together almost every Sunday.

Jobs My Mom Could Do

RYAN

School secretary. Dentist. Waitress. Librarian.
Hairdresser. Teacher. Bus Driver. Nurse.
Eight jobs I can think of where Mom

Could come home every night, instead of working for that
Airline. She's gone too much. We need the
Money, I hear her say. But I wonder if we need
Everything we buy. I'd rather

Have Mom home more
Often, even if it would
Mean we'd have less stuff.
Electrician. Veterinarian. Cook.

Learning to Draw

ASHA

How can Naomi draw like that?
I tried to draw a bird flying in the sky, but

When Natalie looked at it, she said,
How come you put that little check mark
On your cloud? Naomi's birds look almost

Alive, like they could fly off her paper
Right into this room. They're awesome.
Every time I ask her how she does it, she says,

You have to really look at things. I went
Over to her house yesterday and she showed me,
Under a rock, a brown speckled toad. *Look,* she said.
     And I did.

Falcon Soaring High Above
JAQUANNA

We all felt terrible when Monique's father died.
Everyone wanted to cheer her up; we

Just didn't know how. The music teacher
Understood. He helped us write a
Song for the spring concert, dedicated
To Mr. Pirney's memory. Our song is

Called "Falcon Soaring High Above." It tells
About a great, strong bird watching over
Monique, protecting her. In the concert, all of us,
Even Mrs. Williams, stood together

In a semicircle around Monique, singing our song.
Naomi and Asha painted a life-size falcon,

And Mr. Carlson helped Manuel and Andrew make it fly.
Natalie started crying in the middle of the song, but
Dustin sort of stepped in front of

Her until she stopped, so no one noticed. When we finished,
Everyone in the audience stood up, even if they didn't

Know Monique's dad. A lot of people cried, but
Not the bad kind of crying. Since then, it seems like
Everyone's a little different. I think it's that
We're all being nicer to each other.

Green and gold in her
summer dress, Queen Tree dances.
Asha sees her too.

NAOMI

Does She Know?

EDDIE

I wonder what it's like to kiss

Someone. To kiss Veronica.
I wonder if your
Teeth get in the way.

Her hair looks pretty.
Every time I see her
Run across the playground,
Every time she smiles at me, I

Wonder—not that
I want to—I just wonder
Sometimes, about kissing
Her. Does she know
I like her?
No, how could she—
Girls can't read your mind.

One Simple Question

VERONICA

Taste? Lips don't
Have a taste, my sister says. *Don't*
Even think about it!

Please. You're just a
Little kid! Chastity won't
Answer this one simple question.
Come on, she says, *who?*
Eddie, I whisper.

Oh, that skinny kid with a big nose?
No! I yell. *Will you just shut up!*

Mom comes in. *What are*
You two fighting about?

Chastity opens
Her big mouth.
Eddie—that kid that walks by
Every day. Veronica wants to
Kiss him.

River Animals

JACK

Long time ago, the river would
Overflow its banks sometimes, so full
Of fish, ducks, turtles, muskrat, otter.
King of itself, it moved along, no
Stops and starts, no dams like now.

Only dams were made by beavers. We
Used to be friends with
Them. Deer too, and fox. Not

A calendar-law hunting season. Not
The noise of cars and guns. Just a

Time out walking, animals and us, at
Hours of dusk and dawn. The river's U,
Each mile or so, changing year by year. No

Walker sees that now. We drive cars
Over bridges, don't walk along the bank.
River animals must cry sometimes. O
Look what's happened to our home. O
Don't you *see* us? Here and there, so beautiful.

Explorers

JON

Garden Street, past City Market,
Over the old bridge.
I ride out to Jack's house. He grabs his bike and we head
North on Central, out to
Glenwood Park. We leave our bikes

At the entrance to the lake trail. Some days
No one's out there. Sometimes, people fishing.
Yesterday it was just us two.
We walked all the way around the lake. A
Heron landed in the water—we saw it catch a frog,
Eat it, fly away. I counted seven turtles sitting on a log.
Rode home thinking about those great
Explorers, all the things they must have seen.

Spinning Through the Universe

MRS. WILLIAMS

I found out yesterday that I'm expecting twins!

Who will my babies be like? Alert, like
Rosa, quick to react to any
Injustice? Or calm and dreamy, like Naomi? Will
They have to work hard in school, like
Eddie does, or will everything be easy, like it is for Andrew?

Manuel's inventions, or Jaquanna's songs—
You never know what gifts a child will bring. I know, my
        babies

Probably won't grow up to be
Like any of these kids. Every child is like
A little world with ever-changing weather,
Nights and mornings. And somehow, here we are,
Spinning through the universe together.

NOTES ON FORMS

Poetry is made of images, words, music, breathing, ideas, heartbeats, and stories. Many poems are written in free verse, which does not concern itself with given patterns, but the poems in this book are written in poetic forms with patterns such as

—A given number of beats or syllables in every line

—Rhyming words at the ends of certain lines

—Lines repeating in a pattern

—Lines beginning or ending with particular letters

—The end words in the lines repeating in a certain order.

In Part 1, I use a different form for each poem. If there is a conflict between what I imagine the speaker is thinking and what the form demands, I stay true to the speaker's voice, even if it means that I don't follow the exact rules of the form. I may include an extra beat in a line or use a half rhyme or an off rhyme. Such variations can add interest to a poem.

In Part 2, I use the acrostic form (see definition later), taking a phrase from the character's first poem as the armature of the second. (The armature of an acrostic is the line down the side, formed by the letters at the beginning or end of the line.)

You may enjoy trying to figure out the patterns in the poems before reading these notes, something like figuring out a puzzle. When you want to read them, the notes will tell you how the form in each poem works.

Here are a few terms used in describing the forms:

A STANZA is a group of lines. A double space separates two stanzas.

A 2-line stanza is a couplet.

A 3-line stanza is a tercet.

A 4-line stanza is a quatrain.

RHYME is a repeated sound. In these notes it refers to words at the ends of lines. Rhyme is shown by lowercase letters (*a* rhymes with *a*, *b* rhymes with *b*, and so on), unless the rhymed line is also a refrain (see below).

A REFRAIN is a repeated line. It is shown by a capital letter. If the capital letter is the same as a lowercase letter, it means that the refrain rhymes with the line that has the same letter.

An END WORD is the last word of a line. Sometimes end words are repeated in a particular order. End words are shown by lowercase letters.

RHYTHM can be measured in different ways.

–Some forms count SYLLABLES, the separate sounds in a line.

–Some forms count METER, the stressed sounds in a line.

–Different meters have different numbers of short (unstressed) beats for every long (stressed) beat. For example, a common meter is iambic pentameter, a meter in which each line has five segments called FEET, and each foot has one short beat and one long beat. It sounds something like this:

taDUM, taDUM, taDUM, taDUM, taDUM.

NOTES ABOUT THE FORMS IN EACH POEM

GREAT EXPLORERS, ROOM 214 (MRS. WILLIAMS)—**Terza Rima**

Any number of tercets (3-line stanzas).

The first and third lines of each stanza rhyme.

The second line rhymes with the first and third lines of the following stanza.

The poem usually ends with a couplet (2-line stanza); both lines of the couplet rhyme with the middle line of the last tercet.

(Terza rima is usually written in iambic pentameter, but this poem is not.)

ALL OF NAOMI'S POEMS EXCEPT "WHISPERING ABOUT THE TEACHER"—**Haiku**

Three-line poem, with the middle line slightly longer than the first and third. In most of the haiku in this book, I've counted the syllables in each line: 5, 7, 5. Many haiku include images from nature, often showing the seasons.

GRANDMA KEEPS FORGETTING (VONDA)—**Tritina**

Three tercets (3-line stanzas), and one 1-line stanza.

Three words repeat as the end words in the following order:

a, *b*, *c* (end words of stanza 1)

c, *a*, *b* (end words of stanza 2)

b, *c*, *a* (end words of stanza 3)

The last line includes all three end words.

LATE AGAIN (SAM)—**Nonce form**

A nonce form is a form invented by the poet for a particular poem. The form I invented for this poem is:

Three stanzas, each consisting of a rhyming quatrain (4-line stanza) plus a refrain.

Each stanza rhymes *abab*, followed by a refrain with an *A* rhyme.

This pattern is written: *ababA ababA ababA.*

WITHOUT MY BIKE (JON)—**Blank Verse**

Unrhymed lines written in a regular meter, usually, as in this poem, iambic pentameter.

MAKE A FEW ADJUSTMENTS (ANDREW)—**Sestina**

Six 6-line stanzas and one 3-line stanza called an envoi.

Six words (sometimes with slight variations) repeat in a particular order as the end words of each line in each stanza.

The same six words are each used once in the envoi.

The order of the end words (each letter stands for a word) in the 6-line stanzas is: *abcdef, faebdc, cfdabe, ecbfad, deacfb, bdfeca.*

SUKI (RYAN)—**Tanka**

Three lines, followed by two lines, with a given number of syllables in each line:

line 1: 5 syllables
line 2: 7 syllables
line 3: 5 syllables

(Tanka continued)

line 4: 7 syllables

line 5: 7 syllables

This pattern can repeat for as many stanzas as you like. The tanka "Suki" is separated into two parts.

PEPPERONI WAS MY DOG (RICHARD)—**Acrostic**

An acrostic takes a word or phrase (called the armature) and uses it as the beginning, middle, or ending letters of each line. The poem can be about the word or phrase, but it doesn't have to be.

ONE SMALL KITTEN (MANUEL)—**Kyrielle**

Any number of quatrains (4-line stanzas).

The last line of each stanza repeats as a refrain, sometimes with small variations.

The stanzas rhyme *abaB*, *cbcB*, *dbdB*, and so on.

Each line has 8 syllables.

WHO, ME? (JAQUANNA)—**Pantoum**

Any number of quatrains (4-line stanzas).

The second and fourth lines of each stanza repeat as the first and third lines of the following stanza.

The poem can end with the first and third lines of the first stanza repeated in reverse order as a couplet (2-line stanza), so the poem begins and ends with the same line. This rhyme scheme is shown as:

> A1 B1 A2 B2
> B1 C1 B2 C2
> C1 D1 C2 D2
> ...A2 A1

HER THICK BLACK HAIR (LAURA)—Bragi

Two six-line stanzas.

Rhyme:

  stanza 1: *abccba*

  stanza 2: *cbaabc*

Syllables per line: 6, 8, 10, 10, 8, 6, and 10, 8, 6, 6, 8, 10.

So the form requires syllable counts and rhymes together, in this pattern:

LINE	SYLLABLES	RHYME
1	6	*a*
2	8	*b*
3	10	*c*
4	10	*c*
5	8	*b*
6	6	*a*
7	10	*c*
8	8	*b*
9	6	*a*
10	6	*a*
11	8	*b*
12	10	*c*

IT'S HARD TO FIT IN (SHAWNA, KATE, ROSA, NATALIE, CHRYSTAL, MONIQUE, ASHA)—**Crown of Sonnets**

>A sonnet is a 14-line poem, usually written in iambic pentameter.
>
>An Italian sonnet rhymes *abbaabba cdcdcd* or *abbaabba cdecde*.
>
>A crown of sonnets is a set of seven Italian sonnets, linked through repeated lines. The last line of one sonnet is the first line of the next (sometimes with minor variations), and the last line of the last sonnet circles back to the first line of the first sonnet.

RECESS (ANTOINE)—**Quatern**

>A poem written in four quatrains (4-line stanzas).
>
>Line 1 is repeated in each stanza.
>
>In stanza 2 it is line 2.
>
>In stanza 3 it is line 3.
>
>In stanza 4 it is line 4.
>
>Note: "Recess" does not rhyme, but most quaterns do.
>
>The traditional quatern rhyme is: *Abab, bAba, abAb, babA.*

TEN (BEN)—**Villanelle**

>A 19-line poem, with five tercets (3-line stanzas) and one quatrain (4-line stanza).
>
>The first and third lines of each stanza rhyme throughout the poem.
>
>The second lines of each stanza rhyme throughout the poem.

The first and third lines of the first stanza repeat as refrains throughout the poem, alternating as the third line of each stanza (sometimes with slight variations). They are repeated together as the last two lines of the last stanza.

LINE (RHYME)	REFRAIN
A1	refrain
b	
A2	refrain
a	
b	
A1	refrain
a	
b	
A2	refrain
a	
b	
A1	refrain
a	
b	
A2	refrain
a	
b	
A1	refrain
A2	refrain

BOTTOM LINE (DUSTIN)—**Tercelle**

>A 12-line poem in four tercets (3-line stanzas).
>
>The first six lines are mirrored by the last six.
>
>Line 1 repeats as line 12.
>
>Line 2 repeats as line 11.
>
>Line 3 repeats as line 10.
>
>Line 4 repeats as line 9.
>
>Line 5 repeats as line 8.
>
>Line 6 repeats as line 7.

MY PEOPLE (JACK)—**Raccontino**

>Any number of couplets (2-line stanzas).
>
>Even-numbered lines end on the same rhyme.
>
>The title, followed by the last words of the odd-numbered lines, tells a story.

FRIEND (SHARRELL)—**Rondelet**

>A 7-line poem.
>
>The first line is a refrain, repeating as line 3 and again as line 7.
>
>The refrain has 4 syllables, and the other lines have 8 syllables.
>
>Line 4 rhymes with the refrain, and lines 2, 5, and 6 rhyme with one another, in this pattern:

LINE	SYLLABLES	RHYME/REFRAIN
1	4	*A*
2	8	*b*
3	4	*A*
4	8	*a*

(Rondelet continued)

LINE	SYLLABLES	RHYME/REFRAIN
5	8	*b*
6	8	*b*
7	4	*A*

THE TRUTH (MARIA)—Balance

A 20-line poem.

Lines of the same meter rhyme.

Each line uses meter (given here as the number of feet, or stressed sounds) in the following pattern:

LINE	METER	RHYME
1	5	*a*
2	4	*b*
3	3	*c*
4	2	*d*
5	1	*e*
6	1	*e*
7	2	*d*
8	3	*c*
9	4	*b*
10	5	*a*
11	5	*a*
12	4	*b*
13	3	*c*
14	2	*d*
15	1	*e*
16	1	*e*

LINE	METER	RHYME
17	2	*d*
18	3	*c*
19	4	*b*
20	5	*a*

JUST TRY (EDDIE)—Scallop

Three 6-line stanzas, with each line having a particular rhyme and a particular number of syllables.

Syllables per line: 2, 4, 6, 6, 4, 2

Rhyme in each stanza: *abccba*

So, each stanza has the following lines:

LINE	SYLLABLES	RHYME
1	2	*a*
2	4	*b*
3	6	*c*
4	6	*c*
5	4	*b*
6	2	*a*

THE BLUEBIRD ZOO (MATTHEW)—Alphabet Poem

Twenty-six lines of any length.

Each line begins with a different letter, in alphabetical order.

In this poem, the letter X is the second letter of its line.

OUT IN THE HALL (VERONICA)—**Prose Poem**

A poem written in paragraphs instead of stanzas. As in other poems, the language should be lively and include images, and the poet should pay attention to the sounds of the words.

ROOM 214, 11 P.M. (MR. CARLSON)—**Ottava Rima**

A poem of any number of 8-line stanzas.

Each stanza rhymes in this order: *ababbabcc*.

Traditionally, it is written in iambic pentameter, but in this poem the rhythm varies.

All the poems in Part 2, except Naomi's haiku, are *acrostics* (see definition earlier). In these poems, a phrase from the speaker's first poem is the armature for the second poem. In most of the poems, you'll find one armature at the beginnings of the lines (on the left side of the page). But in one poem, there is a double armature, one on the left starting at the top and going down, and the same phrase on the right, starting at the bottom and going up.

To learn more about poetic forms, see *The Teachers & Writers Handbook of Poetic Forms*, 2d ed., edited by Ron Padgett (New York: Teachers & Writers Collaborative, 2000).

ACKNOWLEDGMENTS

The children in this book are fictional. I imagined them and the things they think about. But as I wrote the poems, I remembered many real children I've known. I thank them for being so interesting, intelligent, and basically good at heart. Special thanks to these young readers: Jackson Bloch, Alix and Ian Hudson, Ana and Cara Liuzzi, Ben Mata, RasAmen Oladuwa, Courtney Varner, and the students at Allen County Youth Services Center.

I thank Harvey Cocks, Avon Crismore, Richard and Nora Dauenhauer, Claire Ewart, Alice Friman, Richard Frost, Tom Gephardt, Diana Guzman, Susan Harroff, Gretchen Liuzzi, Barbara Morrow, Ketu Oladuwa, Mary Quigley, April Pulley Sayre, Lola Schaefer, Margaret Schrepfer, Suzanne Scollon, Gail Shears, Ingrid Wendt, Kathryn Willcutt, and members of my SCBWI group for suggestions and encouragement.

I also thank:

Lisa Tsetse and the Fort Wayne Dance Collective, for support in my recent work with children.

The Mary Anderson Center and the Anderson Center at Tower View, for space and time to write.

The Indiana Arts Commission and the National Endowment for the Arts, for support of that writing time.

The Allen County Public Library and the Holiday Inn in Goshen, Indiana, for offering space where writers can meet.

Allison Joseph, for sharing her research on poetic forms invented by women.

Frances Foster, for the gift of her thoughtful, gentle editing, and others at Farrar, Straus and Giroux for all they do to bring each book to completion.

My mother, sisters, brothers, cousins, nieces, nephews, in-laws, and friends, and especially my husband, Chad Thompson, and our sons, Lloyd and Glen, for companionship and love.

Turn the page for

Room 214

bonus materials. . . .

Helen Frost

talks about

Room 214: A Year in Poems

How did you come to write this book?

I wanted to celebrate the fact that children come from so many different homes and situations to create a classroom community.

Are the characters based on real people?

Not exactly. But some of the things that happen in the book have happened to me or to people I know. For example, I thought of the poem "Birthday Candles" when a family I know solved the problem of how to help their son, who had cerebral palsy, blow out the candles on his birthday cake. I loved the idea they came up with—and it worked!

Which character were you most like when you were in fifth grade?

There's a little of myself in each of the characters. When I wrote the series of poems "It's Hard to Fit In," I remembered a situation in fifth grade when a group of girls were teasing a new girl, and I didn't like it, but I didn't stick up for her as I thought I should have. She asked another girl, Kristin, if she would be her friend, and Kristin thought about it and said yes. Since Kristin was well liked, everyone else stopped being mean to the new girl. I've always remembered that, and still think about Kristin when people assume that popular girls are "mean girls." It doesn't have to be so, and often isn't. I was something like Kate in that poem.

Have you ever been a teacher?

Yes. I've taught all the elementary grades in several different kinds of schools, including Kilquhanity House School in Scotland, much like the famous school Summerhill, and a one-teacher school in Telida, Alaska, where I had as few as five students—one in each grade.

The class I taught that was most like Room 214 was a fifth-grade class in Ketchikan, Alaska.

Are you like Mrs. Williams?

Mrs. Williams is based on the teacher I would like to be. When I was teaching, I didn't always measure up to that ideal, so it was nice to write those poems and give this class the teacher they deserve.

How do you pick the names of the characters in your books?

I love all the different names of the children I meet in schools, and I think of them when I name my characters.

How did you decide on the room number?

My aunt Esther was a teacher and a principal for forty years, and her birthday was on Valentine's Day, February 14—or 2/14. That's how I got the idea to use a room number that suggests that this is a classroom centered in love.

Alphabet Poem Worksheet

A poem in which each line begins with a different letter of the alphabet, in alphabetical order. (Note: the letter X is sometimes the second letter of the word for that line.)

A

B

C

D

E

F

G

H

I

J

K

L

M

N

O

P

Q

R

S

T

U

V

W

X

Y

Z

Tercelle Worksheet

Rules of the form:
- A twelve-line poem in four tercets (three line stanzas)
- The first six lines are mirrored by the last six, often with minor variations

Line 1_____

Line 2_____

Line 3_____

Line 4_____

Line 5_____

Line 6_____

──────────── IMAGINARY MIRROR ────────────
IMAGINARY MIRROR

Repeat line 6_____

Repeat line 5_____

Repeat line 4_____

Repeat line 3_____

Repeat line 2_____

Repeat line 1_____

Tritina Worksheet

Rules for form:
- Ten-line poem
- Three 3-line stanzas and one 1-line stanza
- The endwords (last words in the lines) repeat in this pattern:

_____Word A

_____Word B

_____Word C

_____Word C

_____Word A

_____Word B

_____Word B

_____Word C

_____Word A

_____

Words A, B, and C (Use all three words in the last line.)

James and Anikwa have always been the best of friends.
But in a war where their families take opposing sides,
will their friendship remain intact?

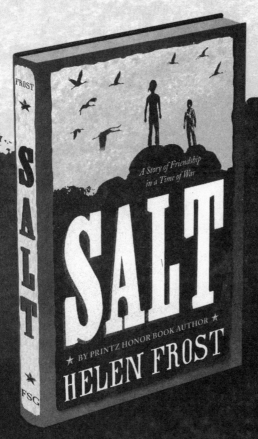

A Story of Friendship
in a Time of War

SALT

★ BY PRINTZ HONOR BOOK AUTHOR ★
HELEN FROST

Turn the page for a sneak peek of
SALT

SALT IN THE SEA, SALT ON THE EARTH

A shallow sea
moves over the earth,
salty, sun-warmed.
Water rises
as mist,
fog, clouds,
leaving a thin coat
of salt on the ground.

JAMES

Dang mosquito bit me right where I can't reach it.
I rub my back against a hickory tree—up and down,

side to side. There—almost got it. Might look silly,
but nobody's watching. Except a squirrel—I hear it

up there in the branches, and I get out my slingshot.
Ma will be happy when I bring home something

for the soup pot. Where is that old squirrel, anyhow?
Sounds like a whole family of 'em, laughing at me,

and I can't see even one. What? Not again! It's
Anikwa, laughing as he jumps down from the tree

and lands beside me. How long has he been watching?
I swear he can sound like anything! Squirrel, bumblebee,

bluebird, or bullfrog. Once, I heard my baby sister crying,
but when I turned to look—it wasn't Molly, it was him!

ANIKWA

James looks
up in the tree like he thinks
there's a real squirrel hiding somewhere
in its branches. I suck in my cheeks
to make myself stop laughing—
he shakes his head,
puts away
his stone and slingshot,
gives me a smile that means I got him
this time, but next time he'll be watching if I
try that trick again. *Come on,* he motions as he heads
to the berry bushes. I've seen him out here picking berries
every afternoon since they started to get ripe.
Makiinkweeminiiki, I say, pretending to
put berries in my mouth and
pointing down the trail
toward the bushes.
He nods his head.
Yes, he says,
blackberries. As we walk
to the berry patch, he tries my word—
makiinkweeminiiki, and I try his—*blackberries.*
I roll both words around like berries
in my mouth.

JAMES

Wonder if my mouth is purple-black, like Anikwa's. I start to head back
up the trail toward home. But wait—what's he saying? *Kiihkoneehsa*—

that means "fish"! He points to the river trail, meaning, *Follow me,* so I do.
When we get to the river, he pulls a string of seven fish out of the water

and gives me a nice-size trout. Wish I knew how he catches all these fish.
Thanks! I say, and then I repeat it in his language: *Neewe.* We walk along

together; I'm happy because he gave me this fish, so I start whistling.
He figures out the tune and whistles along with me. Yesterday, I found

a bee tree full of honey. Wonder if he's seen it. *C'mon,* I motion, *this way.*
It's off the trail a little, past the muddy place. We climb over the big log,

not far from where the trail splits, his trail going to Kekionga, and mine
going back to my house and the fort. Huh? What's that deep hole?

Looks like a person dug it. We step up for a closer look and jump back—
a man we've never seen before is standing in the hole, watching us!

ANIKWA

When I get home,
Grandma's cutting deer meat
into strips she's hanging on the drying rack.
I show her the fish I caught. She smiles.
Some for now, and some to salt
and save for winter.
We'll need more
salt before too long, she says.
Grandma, I say, *I saw a man.* She looks up.
Standing in a hole, I tell her, *near where the trail divides.*
He's not from here. Do you know who he is? She thinks about it.
I saw an Ojibwe man walking on that trail yesterday, she says. *Maybe*
he wants to see what's happening here. She doesn't seem scared.
She needs more hickory wood—her fire's almost out—
so I say, *Toontwa, let's get firewood for Grandma.*
Toontwa likes to eat—a lot—but he doesn't
like to carry firewood. *I saw foxes*
playing behind the big rock,
I tell him. *We could*
look for their den. That gets him
interested. *How many?* he asks. *Five,* I say.
I pick up my wood-carrying basket and walk off.
He follows with his basket like I
hoped he would.

JAMES

Ma asks, *What did you see today?* I tell her about a dead turtle in the creek, and a tree that fell across the trail, but I don't mention the man, or the hole

he must've dug. Ma might get worried and say I can't go out by myself. She's cutting up the fish when Pa comes in and sits down at the table.

Look what James brought home! she says. *Nice-looking trout,* says Pa. *Where did you catch it, Son?* I could pretend I caught it. But I know better than to

lie to Pa. That's one thing he won't abide. *Anikwa caught it,* I admit. Ma says, *Next time his aunt and uncle come to trade, give them a little extra.*

Ma calls Mink and Old Raccoon Anikwa's aunt and uncle, but Anikwa calls Old Raccoon his father. From what I can tell, Miami children

have a lot of parents. That's good if your ma and pa die, like his did. His mother died of smallpox when he was two years old, and then

a year later, his father got killed. *In a skirmish,* Pa said. *That's like a war, but smaller.* Makes me wonder: Who'd take care of me if Pa and Ma died?

ANIKWA

This lacrosse stick
is too big for me, but I like to use it
because it was my father's. Grandma tells me,
He was the best lacrosse player I ever saw.
He was so good, he could
make it seem like his
younger brother
was as good as he was.
I wish I remembered him better.
They say his voice was like strong music.
Everyone loved to listen to him speak. When people
started arguing, he said what he thought, and then stayed quiet
while other people spoke. People listened to him, and thought
carefully about anything he said. *His words,* Father says,
rose to the top, when we had to make hard decisions
about war or treaties—what to do
when all the changes came
across our land.
At first,
new kinds of sickness, then
a different kind of people—starting with men,
who soon brought families. Then soldiers, and the fort.
Like the bees that flew in from the east
and settled on our flowers.

JAMES

I'm going out fishing, alone, when here comes Isaac: *Where you going?* Dang.
I was hoping to catch a lot of fish and give one to Anikwa. I never see him

when Isaac's with me. Don't want to be mean, so I tell Isaac where I'm headed.
He walks along beside me, talking, talking, talking. *There's gonna be a war here.*

Not sure I'm supposed to tell you. Your pa and ma might not want you to know.
Like he's old enough to know about it, and I'm not—I'm older than he is!

Course I heard about it, I say, even though I haven't. I keep quiet, hoping
he'll say more, and he does: *My pa says the Indians are on the British side.*

That can't be true. *You don't know what you're talking about,* I blurt out.
They've been our friends since Ma was a girl. Her grandpa traded with them!

He shakes his head. *I know what I'm talking about, but you don't,* he says.
I bet you don't even know about the siege. I shrug, like I know but I don't care.

The Indians might block the fort, he says, *so we can't get out until the British come.*
Then they'll all join up and attack us. Trying to act like he knows everything.

ANIKWA

Kwaahkwa
and I came to this quiet
place to fish. We listen to the river
whisper in that soft, low voice
it has sometimes. There's
a pair of bluebirds
singing
on a low branch of the oak.
Two fish arc out of the water near
the eddy, showing us exactly where they are.
Then, over by that sycamore that fell last year, a big
bullfrog starts up talking like a drum. I answer, and he
answers back. And then we hear something else—
James's quiet voice, Isaac's scratchy loud one.
It sounds like they're arguing. Everything
except the river and the frog stops
talking. The bluebirds fly
away, the ducks dive
underwater.
We move into the shadows,
crouch down behind a rock, and watch.
Not exactly hiding, just staying quiet, listening
and keeping our eyes
open.

JAMES

Isaac keeps trying to show off how much he knows. *Don't worry, James,*
he says (he thinks I'm scared), *the Americans might get here first. Pa told me*

our army is bigger than the British army. But if the Indians join the British,
we're done for. He slices his hand across his throat. I know how to scare him:

lead him past the hole I saw when I was with Anikwa. If that man's still
standing in it, Isaac will jump out of his skin. Better not, though. He'd tell

his ma, and she'd tell mine, and they'd make us stay inside the stockade
where they could keep an eye on us. I'd hate that. We're walking by the river,

near where Anikwa gave me the fish, when Isaac comes to a sudden stop.
Look! He points. *Over there by that tree!* He picks up a rock and throws it

as hard as he can. *I think I hit it!* He runs over, leans down, and holds up
a dead bullfrog, so proud of himself. *Isaac,* I ask, *what'd you do that for?*

That frog didn't hurt you. He stares at me. *For fun,* he says. *How come you*
never like to have fun? I look around—I sure hope Anikwa isn't watching.

ANIKWA

Splash!

The frog stops talking.

Did it jump out of the way in time?

Did it sink down in the mud?

Or—did that rock hit it?

I lean back so I can

see: Isaac

lifts the bullfrog

from the water at the river's edge.

The frog's legs (strong enough to cross a creek

in two jumps) dangle from his hands. Isaac smiles like

he's in a war against the frogs and he just won a battle. I grab

a rock to throw at *him*, but Kwaahkwa says, *You know*

frogs taste good. That boy gets hungry, just like us.

Then Isaac swings the bullfrog by its legs,

around and around, over his head.

He's about to throw it

in the deep part

of the river.

No one will have that frog

for supper. I jump up and run to try

to stop him, or catch the frog, but it goes flying

through the air just before I

grab Isaac's arm.

JAMES

Isaac and Anikwa slip in the mud and end up in the river. I didn't see which one pushed first, but they could both get pulled downriver.

Who should I help? I pick up a long branch and lie down on the bank to hold it out. Isaac reaches it first—he grabs it and pulls himself up.

Anikwa is still in the water, sputtering from all the water in his nose (and because he's mad about that frog, I bet). I don't see Kwaahkwa

coming until he reaches out to Anikwa, pulls him out of the water, and starts talking fast—not sure what they're saying, but it looks

like Anikwa would push Isaac back in the river if Kwaahkwa didn't stop him. Anikwa takes off his moccasins, squeezes out the water, and

puts them back on, glaring at Isaac the whole time. He walks away with Kwaahkwa, glancing at the river where the dead frog floats downstream.

Isaac shakes himself like a dog trying to get dry. *See?* he says to me. *That boy just attacked me for no reason! I told you they're not on our side.*

Discover the world of
HELEN FROST

978-0-312-64127-6

A Printz Honor award winner

978-0-312-60383-0

"Blends exciting survival adventure with a contemporary girl's discovery of family roots and secrets." —*BOOKLIST*

978

"This poe
to
A
—S
Kids Ink

10-14